PETER POWERS™

and the Itchy Insect Invasion!

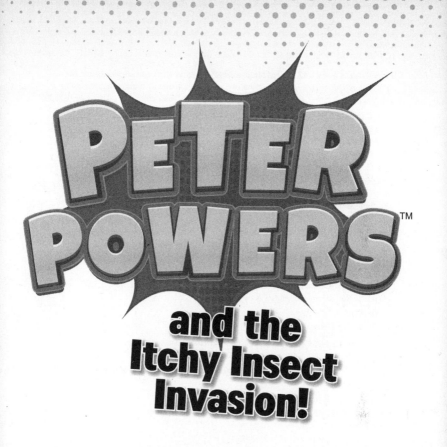

PETER POWERS™

and the Itchy Insect Invasion!

**By Kent Clark
& Brandon T. Snider
Art by Dave Bardin**

Little, Brown and Company

New York Boston

Copyright © 2017 by Hachette Book Group, Inc.
PETER POWERS is a trademark of Hachette Book Group.
Cover and interior art by Dave Bardin
Cover design by Christina Quintero
Cover copyright © 2017 by Hachette Book Group, Inc.

Little, Brown and Company
Hachette Book Group
1290 Avenue of the Americas, New York, NY 10104
Visit us at lb-kids.com

First Edition: March 2017

Little, Brown and Company is a division of Hachette Book Group, Inc.
The Little, Brown name and logo are trademarks of Hachette Book Group, Inc.

The publisher is not responsible for websites (or their content) that are not owned by the publisher.

Library of Congress Cataloging-in-Publication Data
Names: Clark, Kent, author. | Snider, Brandon T., author. | Bardin, Dave (Illustrator), illustrator.
Title: Peter Powers and the itchy insect invasion! / by Kent Clark & Brandon T. Snider ; art by Dave Bardin.
Description: First edition. | New York ; Boston : Little, Brown and Company, 2017. | Series: Peter Powers ; [3] | Summary: "Peter Power overcomes his fear of bugs in order to save his family from Spidra and Bug Master." —Provided by publisher.
Identifiers: LCCN 2016028465 | ISBN 9780316359474 (hardback) | ISBN 9780316359498 (e-book) | ISBN 9780316359436 (library edition e-book)
Subjects: | CYAC: Superheroes—Fiction. | Ability—Fiction. | Family life—Fiction. | Fear—Fiction. | Insects—Fiction. | Humorous stories. | BISAC: JUVENILE FICTION / Action & Adventure / General. | JUVENILE FICTION / Humorous Stories. | JUVENILE FICTION / Readers / Chapter Books.
Classification: LCC PZ7.1.C594 Pd 2017 | DDC [Fic]—dc23
LC record available at https://lccn.loc.gov/2016028465

ISBNs: 978-0-316-35947-4 (hardcover), 978-0-316-54358-3 (pbk.),
978-0-316-35949-8 (ebook)

Printed in the United States of America

LSC-C

Hardcover: 10 9 8 7 6 5 4 3 2 1
Paperback: 10 9 8 7 6 5 4 3 2 1

Contents

CHAPTER ONE
Battle at the School

"Students, get away from the windows!" Miss Dullworth shouted. But no one listened. Everyone in the classroom was huddled at the windows.

Outside, two of the world's greatest superheroes were fighting a super-villainess on the front lawn of my school. Little did the other students know that those superheroes are *my parents*.

I wanted to go out there and help.

Instead, I was stuck inside watching it all happen. Talk about *boring*.

Who am I? I'm Peter Powers. And I'm on the verge of becoming the greatest super-hero the world has ever known! Well, kind of. You might need to give me a few years.

"Look at them go!" I cheered.

As the fearless protectors of Boulder City, my parents were always the first on the scene to help. Dad controls fire, and

Mom can fly faster than a rocket. They're both super tough.

Today, they were battling a nasty criminal named Spidra. The masked crook was tearing the schoolyard apart with her eight hairy spider limbs! The whole bug look? Totally creeps me out.

Did I mention that I'm deathly afraid of bugs? (Just saying the word makes me start itching all over.)

The entire classroom was glued to the windows, watching my parents take down Spidra. No one knows about my super-powered family, except Chloe and Sandro. They're my best friends in the entire universe.

"Your mom is pretty *and* awesome," Sandro whispered, making his eyebrows jump up and down.

"My dad is pretty rad too," I said. "He makes great burgers at family barbecues."

Chloe pinched Sandro and me. "You guys shouldn't talk about this here," she whispered. "Secret identities, remember? You don't want to blow your parents' cover."

She was right, of course. Chloe is pretty much a super know-it-all.

"Just think, Peter. Someday you'll be a big superhero fighting some nutty bad guy," Sandro said. "You'll probably get so famous you'll forget about us."

"I'll never forget about you two," I said. "Even *if* I do become a famous superhero."

"You mean *when* you become one," Chloe said with a wink.

Chloe was right. But it's going to take a lot of work before I get there. I do have superpowers, so that's a start. They're not much, but I'm working on them. I can create ice cubes with my fingers. I can freeze other stuff too! Well, sometimes. It's not glamorous, but I can definitely keep a drink cold in the summer. I'm learning how to do more stuff, but it's taking *forever*.

"Check out your dad!" Chloe whispered, pointing out the window.

"I've had quite enough of your antics, Spidra!" Dad said, firing off a wall of flame.

"You'll never take me, do-gooders!" Spidra shouted, shooting webs with

 her sticky-icky spider fingers. Just seeing it made me queasy.

"Oh, yes

we will," Mom said, swooping down from the sky and knocking Spidra out. Then Mom grabbed her by the collar and flew her to jail.

"That's going to be me one day," I whispered.

"You want to be a weirdo spider lady?" asked Sandro. Chloe and I shook our heads. Sandro stared blankly until he figured it out. "Oh! You mean you want to be like your mom and dad. Okay, that makes more sense."

Dad looked over and gave me a thumbs-up. He and Mom weren't afraid of *anything*.

I couldn't wait to be just like them.

CHAPTER TWO
Breakfast Bug

"Slow down, honey. Breakfast is not a race," my mom said.

Gavin, my older brother, sat at the breakfast table, stuffing his face with waffles as fast as he could. Footsteps raced down the stairs. Another Gavin ran into the kitchen and snatched the waffles from his clone. "Beat it, dupe! Those are my waffles!"

Gavin snapped his fingers, and the clone Gavin vanished. Oh yeah, Gavin has the power to create duplicates of himself. But sometimes they do their own thing.

"Gavin, *no clones at the breakfast table*. How many times do I have to tell you?" Mom said. Gavin wasn't listening. He was already chowing down on another buttery waffle.

"Mom, can I go *out* later?" my little sister, Felicia, asked.

"Where do you want to go?" Mom said.

"I just want to go *out!* Jeez, Mom, why are you always in my business?" Felicia whined, banging her fist on the table. A crack formed in the wood. Felicia is super strong. She's always breaking things around the house.

"Focus on your breakfast. We can discuss the rest once you're home from school," said Mom. Felicia sighed, poking at her eggs.

"*Geeeeee!*" gurgled my baby brother, Ben. Mom strapped him into his high chair and wiped the slobber from his chin. He has powers too: Ben can turn invisible. Which makes babysitting a nightmare. For now, he was happy chewing on his fingers.

"Good job capturing Spidra yesterday, Mom!" I said. "You and Dad are so confident out there. It's really inspiring."

"Thank you, Peter," Mom said. "Did *you* want something too?"

"Just to be a superhero," I said. "I've been watching your battles on the Internet. If I want to learn how to be a hero, I've got to study from the best."

My mom blushed. "Aren't you full of compliments today!"

"Brownnosers smell," Felicia said with a smirk. "Do you know what they smell like?"

"That smell is just your breath blowing back in your face," I said.

"Play nice, you two," my mom said.

I lifted a forkful of waffle to my mouth. But just as I was about to open wide, I saw a giant bug sitting quietly on my waffle.

"BUG!!!" I screamed, accidentally spraying ice all over the kitchen with my hands. Gavin and Felicia laughed and high-fived.

"What is going on?!" Mom exclaimed.

"I didn't mean to!" I said, starting to itch uncontrollably. "Lately, when I get nervous or scared, my ice power goes crazy. Sorry."

Gavin was laughing so hard, he fell out of his chair. "Ha-ha-ha-ha-ha! I put a fake plastic bug on Peter's waffle!"

"Gavin, you're grounded," Mom growled.

"What?! Why? It's not my fault Peter is afraid of bugs!" Gavin complained. "If some icky, sticky creepy-crawly was on *my* waffle, I wouldn't freak out!"

"Excuse yourself from the table," Mom ordered. "You know what you did was wrong."

Gavin got up and left the table in a huff. Meanwhile, I was still half-itching, half-paralyzed by the fact that I almost ate an insect.

"Sorry about the ice everywhere," I said.

"It's fine. Ice is just cold water. But do you want to talk about your power explosion?" asked Mom.

"I do NOT like bugs, and I do NOT want to talk about it," I said.

"Well, if you don't want to talk to me, maybe talk to Grandpa Dale," Mom said.

Mom's dad is the only person in the house who actually understands me. Grandpa used to be a famous superhero too, but he retired. He's in a wheelchair now, but every once in a while, he'll get up and fly around the house with his big wings.

"Speaking of Grandpa, where is he?" I asked. "He never misses breakfast."

"He's sleeping," Mom replied. "He had a late night out with his bingo buddies."

"Why can't *I* play bingo?" groaned Felicia, getting up from the table and stomping off.

"Never a dull moment at our house," Mom said. "Let's clean up all this ice and then get you kids to school."

CHAPTER THREE
Diving Board Blues

"Nice trunks, Powers!" Harry Hackney shouted from across the pool. He always has something rude to say about everything. Ugh, that guy is *the worst*.

Of course, I did forget to bring my

swim trunks, so I had to borrow some from the lost-and-found bin. They had big pink hearts on them. *Whatever*. At least I wasn't wearing a Speedo.

"Blow it out your nosehole, Hackney!" I shouted back. Did I really just say that? Yes. *Yes, I did.* Sometimes my mouth says things that get me in trouble.

But I wasn't about to let Harry Hackney or my forgetfulness ruin the excitement of the school's new *pool!* Usually, gym class was all about me getting dodgeballs thrown in my face, but not this time. *This* time, I was going to show off my amazing swimming skills. The new pool even had a twelve-foot-high diving board! The class was going to freak out when they saw me up there! I've got some pretty killer form.

"Are you ready to do this?" Chloe asked.

"Chloe, I was *born* ready," I answered.

"Hey, guys!" Sandro said, strutting out of the locker room. He was wearing an itty-bitty Speedo.

"Did you forget your trunks too?" I asked.

"No, why? Oh, you mean these tight little guys? I brought them from home," said Sandro. He slapped his belly and smiled. "I look *good*, right?"

"Ha-ha! Check out Sandro in his little Speedo!" Harry Hackney cackled.

"Blow it out your nosehole, Hackney!" said Sandro. (So *that's* where I got my insult.) "Ugh, that guy is the worst."

"LINE UP, PIGLETS! AND NO

RUNNING!" screamed our gym teacher, Coach Winterbottom. He always calls us farm animals. I guess when you've been a gym teacher for a long time, it can get pretty boring.

Chloe, Sandro, and I got in line with the other students. Harry Hackney and his buddies pushed their way through, cutting in front of everyone. If there is one thing I despise, it's a line cutter. Maybe it was time to teach Hackney a lesson and put an ice cube down his pants....

"*Peter*," Chloe whispered. "I know that look in your eye. Whatever you're thinking about doing—*don't*. It's not worth it."

She was right. I couldn't ruin my secret

identity over something so silly. Harry Hackney wasn't worth it.

Hackney and his friends jumped, and then Chloe and Sandro jumped, and then it was my turn. I was so excited, I rushed up the ladder.

But when I got to the top, all of a sudden my legs weren't moving. I stood there shivering like a Chihuahua in the rain. The diving board was TWELVE FEET IN THE AIR. That suddenly seemed like a *lot* of feet. Then I remembered that *I'm afraid of heights*.

But as I looked around, the whole class was watching. Hackney and his goons were pointing and whispering at me. I

had to
jump!
I put
one foot in
front of the other and
made my way toward
my doom. Each step
felt like an eternity.

I gripped the railing
so tightly that I thought
I was going to crush it
like my sister could. I
looked down at Chloe
and Sandro, who gave
me two thumbs up. But
once I was at the edge

of the board, vertigo hit me. I got so dizzy that my eyes began to blur and I felt like I was going to throw up.

"I can't," I said. Before I knew what I was doing, I was climbing down the ladder.

First, I heard giggles. Those giggles then turned into full-blown laughter. Soon the whole class was cackling at me— except for Chloe and Sandro, of course.

"Don't worry, Peter," said Chloe. "You'll get it next time."

Yeah, I thought, *sure I will.* At that moment, life sure did stink.

CHAPTER FOUR
Bug Break

"All right, class," Miss Dullworth said. "Today, we will be looking at insects."

Wait a minute. Insects?! No way. Nuh-uh. I didn't want ANY part of THAT. I put my head down, closed my eyes, and wished my superpower was teleporting so I could teleport home.

"*Pssst,*" Chloe whispered. "You're not still thinking about the whole diving thing, right?"

"I wasn't, but I am *now!*" I s

and heights in the same day? Today is the worst!"

"Don't be so hard on yourself," Chloe said. "You've faced supervillains."

"Yeah, and today, I couldn't even handle a diving board!"

"That was just a blip on the radar. You're a fearless superhero who is going to *crush* the competition one day," Chloe assured me. If you haven't noticed, she's *really* good at pep talks.

"Chloe, have you ever thought about becoming an inspirational speaker?" I asked.

"Did someone say inspirational *squeaker*?" Sandro chimed in, letting out a tiny fart.

Miss Dullworth placed a glass terrarium on her desk. It was covered with a scarf, which meant that underneath it was BUGS. I began to squirm in my seat.

"There's nothing to worry about, Peter," Chloe said. "Bugs are just bugs."

"Ready, class?" Miss Dullworth said, smiling and rubbing her hands together. *She* was loving this, but *I* sure wasn't.

"I'm not!" I said, surprisingly. *That* thought was supposed to stay in my head.

"Oh really, Mr. Powers?" asked Miss Dullworth. "Will you let us know when you *are* ready?"

I looked at Chloe for help. She nodded at me—but what did her nod mean? The room stayed silent for a good ten seconds, with everyone waiting on me. "Okay, fine!" I said. "I'm ready right now."

"Good," said Miss Dullworth, grabbing the scarf and whipping it off the terrarium. "Gaze

upon THE JERUSALEM CRICKET!"

The class gathered to watch the bug hop

around. Unable to help myself, I became itchy all over. I hung toward the back because bugs are freaky and frightening. I mean, they look like aliens! This one looked like a huge, brown bee whose wings were replaced by crazy legs.

"Is it poisonous?" I asked.

"No, Peter. I wouldn't bring a creature into the classroom that had the ability to harm anyone," Miss Dullworth said. "Now, can anyone tell me about the Jerusalem cricket?"

Chloe began speaking so quickly, it was like she was possessed by an information demon. "Well, they're found mostly in the western United States and parts of Mexico. Its bite might hurt, but don't worry, it's not venomous. For a meal, the Jerusalem cricket enjoys eating dead insects. And they're flightless."

"Just like me!" I said. Once again, a thought had escaped my brain and traveled to my mouth a little too early.

"Quiet, class. And listen closely," Miss Dullworth said.

THUMP! THUMP! THUMP! THUMP!

We heard what sounded like drumming—and it was coming from the terrarium. "The cricket communicates by rubbing its legs together," said Miss Dullworth.

"Ugh, Sandro, did you fart again?" someone asked. "It stinks in here!"

"No way!" said Sandro. "I *always* claim my farts. Well, most of them."

Miss Dullworth was not amused. "What you are smelling is the Jerusalem cricket. It emits a foul smell whenever it feels threatened," she said.

"So, it feels…threatened?" I asked, backing away slowly. My mom said that when animals and humans feel

threatened, sometimes they react without thinking. I'm not a scientist, but that *can't* be good.

"It's probably a little scared. There's an entire classroom of students crowding around it," explained Miss Dullworth.

"That sounds dangerous," I said, shaking my head.

Harry Hackney leaned in so close, his face was pressed right up against the

glass. He stared at the cricket like he was going to eat it. "BOO!" he yelled.

The cricket jumped out of the terrarium, ripping through the lid! It hopped around the classroom, chasing Miss Dullworth. She screamed. Students ran in every direction, diving under desks and jumping on top of them. I stood in the middle of it all, frozen with fear, watching the chaos around me.

The cricket bit Miss Dullworth right on the butt as she flailed her arms in every direction. But that's not even the craziest part. The cricket

made a break for it. It launched itself into the air and crashed through the window, causing the glass to shatter into a million pieces. Clearly it was no ordinary bug.

When the chaos ended, Miss Dullworth stood there in a daze. No one uttered a word. No one except *me*, of course.

"Told you so," I said. The bell rang and I got out of there as quick as I could.

CHAPTER FIVE
Bingo, Bells, and Bugs

"Bye, losers!" Felicia said, throwing open the front door.

"Stop right there!" Gavin said. "All three of us are stuck on Ben-babysitting duty. You're not going anywhere!"

"Who's going to stop me?" my sister said.

"You'll stop yourself," I said, "unless you want us to tell Mom and Dad, who will ground you for life."

She paused for a moment, then grumpily

closed the door. She threw herself on the couch. "What are we watching?"

"Our new favorite show: *Puppy Justice*. It's about puppies who are also lawyers. It's totally hilarious," I said.

"Dumb," she moaned.

Dealing with my little sister's drama wasn't usually my job. But Mom and Dad were in another dimension, battling some crazy tentacle monster that was going to eat the omniverse, or something. Their adventures all run together after a while.

"BANGO BONGO BINGO!" Grandpa yelled, rocketing through the house in his wheelchair. He put on his fancy hat and said, "Off to bingo. Don't wait up."

"Grandpa, are you sure you don't want to stay with us?" I asked. Dealing with my brothers and sister was always easier with him around. "We can watch all the old black-and-white movies you love. I'll make popcorn!"

Grandpa shook his head. "Nah, the popcorn gets stuck in my teeth."

"So just take them out," I said. Grandpa Dale loved taking out his false teeth and putting them on my shoulder when I wasn't looking. It was hysterical.

"No can do, kiddo.

TONIGHT IS MY NIGHT! I'm going to win *big*. I can feel it in my wings," Grandpa said, wheeling over to the front door and stopping in front of Felicia, who was now standing in his way. "Where do you think you're going, missy?"

"If you're going out, so am I!" said Felicia, staring down Grandpa. It was a standoff!

"No, you're not. You're nine years old. The only place for you on a school night is in your room doing homework," said Grandpa. "That, and keeping an eye on your little brother—who, by the looks of it, you three dunces have already lost. Good luck finding invisible Ben."

Grandpa waved as he closed the door
behind him.

"WHY?!" Felicia wailed, falling to her
knees as if she was the main character
in a very serious play. "WHY DOES THIS
ALWAYS HAPPEN TO ME?!" There weren't
any tears, so Gavin and I just
ignored her.

"Where is Ben?" I asked
Gavin.

He clapped his hands,
and ten duplicates appeared.

"Time to find Ben
again!" Gavin commanded.
His duplicates split up and
scoured the house. Before

37

we knew it, the duplicates found Ben and delivered him right to the couch.

"We need a way to keep track of him," said Felicia. "Maybe a leash?"

"Don't be mean," I said. But she did have a point. Since Ben can turn invisible, we always lose track of him. Not this time. This time, I had a plan. "To the junk drawer!"

Felicia's and Gavin's eyes widened. We ran to the kitchen, pulled out the junk drawer, and placed it on the living room floor. We dug through it like it was treasure. Our family junk drawer was filled with trinkets, office supplies, and mystery items—everything you could imagine.

"What are we looking for?" Gavin asked.

"Bells would be good," I said. "We'll tie them together and make a bracelet for Ben. That way, no matter where he goes, we'll hear him." We dug into the pile of junk like animals. I knew this was a good plan, especially because I'd gotten Felicia and Gavin to work together. They didn't even complain! Darn, I'm good.

After twenty minutes, we'd found ten

different-sized bells. We tied them together and slipped them onto Ben's wrist. He gave it a jangle. Yep, it was loud, all right. Now even if Ben turned invisible, we'd still hear him. Not too shabby.

BBBBBZZZZZZZZZZZZ!

"Those bells sound weird," Felicia said.

"I don't think that was the bells," I said.

Something was happening outside. The humming got louder and louder, almost like a giant lawn mower. As I threw open the curtains, I screamed. My worst nightmare had come true.

Giant swarms of flying insects were covering the city like big, gross clouds.

"BUGS!!!!" I yelled. A news bulletin interrupted *Puppy Justice* and flashed across the TV screen.

"An infestation of insects has gripped the city. Police ask that you stay inside your homes," the news anchor declared. "Close all windows and doors, and hope that they do not get inside."

I trembled at the thought. My whole body became super itchy. I scratched and scratched and scratched, but it didn't help.

"Ha! Peter is afraid of bugs!" Gavin laughed.

Then Felicia joined in. "Don't worry, Peter. I'm sure the bugs are totally

uninterested in the crumbs left in your
bed from all your late-night snacking!"

How did she know I ate in bed late at
night? I don't do it all the time, only when
I'm starving. I didn't even think about
crumbs attracting bugs!

THOOM! THOOM! THOOM!

We all gazed out the window in disbelief.

A giant bug—over
one hundred feet
tall—was walking
right down the
street! Gavin
gulped. Felicia
freaked. Me? I
fainted.

CHAPTER SIX
A Snack for Grandpa

SNAP. SNAP. SNAP.

I heard someone snapping their fingers, trying to wake me up.

"No, like this, Grandpa," Gavin said. Then he slapped me. *SLAP!*

"*Ow!* I'm awake," I said groggily. "What happened?"

"You fainted," Felicia said.

"I did?" I asked. Then I remembered. There were bugs in the sky and a giant bug stomping through the streets. And fainting made sense. "Where'd the bugs go?!"

"I chased them off when I came home to check on you," said Grandpa.

That wasn't very reassuring. Then he leaned in and whispered. "You're going to have to learn to overcome your fears if you want to be a world-class superhero. Trust me on this one."

Grandpa was right. I just wish I knew how to do that. Fear is...well, scary!

"Aw, man. That was totally hilarious. Peter passed out cold and drooled all over himself!" Gavin told Grandpa.

"You two were scared too!" I shouted at my brother and sister.

"*Geeeeee!*" said Ben, smiling in the corner. If *he* was okay, I could relax a little bit. Or so I thought.

THUMP! THUMP! THUMP! THUMP!

"STOP EVERYTHING!" I exclaimed. Grandpa, Gavin, and Felicia paused to listen.

THUMP! THUMP! THUMP! THUMP!

I knew that drumming sound. It was coming from *inside* the house. I scanned the area, looking for the source. That's when I saw it. *Why are all my nightmares coming true?* I thought.

"NASTY INSECT ALERT!" I screamed, jumping up on the couch and pointing to the bug on the coffee table. Grandpa

giggled and shook his head like it wasn't
a big deal.

"Calm down, Peter," Grandpa said.
"I've got this."

He locked eyes with the cricket. It was
a total stare-down. I think Grandpa even
growled at one point. Then he did something
even *I* didn't expect. He opened his mouth,
and out came the longest tongue I'd ever

seen! It snatched the cricket and rolled right back into Grandpa's mouth, lickety-split.

Grandpa started chewing. "What are you looking at? I'm hungry!" Grandpa said, crunching on the cricket.

"GRANDPA!" Gavin shouted, covering his mouth as though he might hurl.

"That is so many levels of gross!" Felicia groaned.

"What?" Grandpa asked. "Insects are full of protein! We'll all be eating them one day—if they don't end up taking over our planet."

"If bugs take over the world, you'll find Peter in the corner, crying like a baby," Gavin said with a grin.

I'd had just about enough of him making fun of me. "There's no way bugs will ever take over—because I won't ever let that—" I started. In the middle of my speech, a bright light shone through the window and blinded me. I tripped over my own foot and fell down. My brother and sister started laughing at me.

"Shut it, you two," Grandpa commanded. "Look!"

We went to the window to see what was happening. Millions of fireflies were soaring up into the sky to form giant letters. They spelled out a dangerous warning:

"Well," Grandpa said, letting out a long sigh. *"That's* not good."

CHAPTER SEVEN
Spider Test

"I can't eat this," I said, pushing away my fruit salad. "The raisins look like insects. Everywhere I look, all I see are BUGS."

"I've been thinking about your whole fear-of-bugs thing," Chloe said from across the cafeteria table. "What if it's actually easy to overcome?"

"*Hmmm*," I said quizzically. "Explain."

"It's like this: My aunt Bertha is really afraid of costumed characters," Chloe revealed. "*Don't* tell her I told you."

"You mean like someone dressed up in a bear costume?" I asked. "What's scary about that?"

"Are you kidding me, Peter? Bears are *terrifying*! They're not as smiley and cuddly as cartoons would have you believe," she said. "Now imagine a human being putting on a smiling bear costume and trying to hug you."

It *did* seem kind of freaky when she said it like that.

"What did your aunt Bertha do to conquer her fear?" I asked.

"She got a job at a costume store. That way she was around costumed characters all the time. Instead of being more afraid, it made her see just how *un*-scary they really were."

"That makes sense," I said. "But what do I do? I'm NOT getting a job in a bug store!"

"No, silly. Bugs are part of nature, and they're never going away. So make peace with them. The more you have to deal

with bugs in your everyday life, the sooner your fear will go away."

Everything she said made sense. "Chloe, you're a GENIUS!"

"Turn the volume down a notch, Peter," she said. "People are staring."

"I think this is a great plan," I whispered. "It's also a *very scary* plan."

"It might be scary, but that's okay. When we're through? It won't be scary anymore," Chloe assured me. She had a really good way of telling me the truth, even when I didn't want to hear it.

"Hey, guys!" said Sandro, plopping his tray down and digging into his mashed potatoes. "Are you talking about that crazy bug swarm that covered the city? It was *totally disgusting*, right? Bug Master is the WORST. Even worse than Spidra—and she's pretty bad. Some people are saying the army of bugs is still out there hiding in the walls, in the trees, and underground. So many creepy-crawlies just waiting to strike! Scary, huh?"

My skin was itchy just thinking about it. Now I had bugs on the brain again. Ugh!

"Peter, you're not eating your lunch," Sandro said with his mouth full of mushy potatoes. "Lunch is the most precious meal of the day."

"All this bug talk made me lose my appetite."

Chloe wasn't about to give up on me. "Eat, Peter! You're going to need all your strength if you want to conquer your fears."

Sandro caught on. "Ohhhh. Is Peter going to try and get over his fear of bugs? That's awesome!" he said, slapping me on the back. "Don't worry, buddy. We promise to do whatever it takes to help you out!"

• • • • • ● • • • • •

Later, in class, I was thinking about what Chloe said. It was going to take a lot of hard work, but she was right. There was no way around it. Thankfully, I had two awesome friends who always had my back. I felt like the luckiest guy in the world—until Sandro put a spider on my shoulder.

"*Shhh*, don't scream," he whispered. "Consider it a test."

I felt that thing crawling on me, and I wanted to yell or scratch or freak out. Instead, I was frozen with fear. Suddenly, I felt a tingle in my fingertips, and knew I was in trouble. My ice powers!

PLOP! PLOP PLOP! PLOP PLOP PLOP!

Tiny ice cubes began shooting out of my fingers, covering the floor below my desk. All because of an itsy-bitsy little spider.

"Sandro!" Chloe hissed. "Stop!"

Sandro put the spider back in his pocket, but the damage was done. There were ice cubes everywhere.

Miss Dullworth looked up. "Who spilled their drink? Ice on the floor is *very* dangerous. Someone could slip and hurt themselves! Who did this?" she asked.

Chloe looked at Sandro. Sandro looked at me. I looked at Miss Dullworth. No one said anything.

"Don't want to tell me who, huh? Very well. But clean it up!" Miss Dullworth said, handing us a roll of paper towels.

"*That* was a close one," Sandro whispered.

"It's going to be okay, Peter," Chloe said. "You're going to beat your fears. Trust me on this."

I wanted to trust Chloe. I really did. But was she right?

CHAPTER EIGHT
Parent Patrol

"Hey, buddy. How's it going?" Dad asked, poking his head into my bedroom.

"It's going," I said.

"Trying to shake this whole fear thing, huh? We all have fears, son. It's nothing to be ashamed of," Dad said, taking a seat next to me on my bed. "I was afraid of *everything* when I was your age. Even stuff that I knew couldn't hurt me."

"Oh yeah? Like what?" I asked.

"When I was little, I used to think the

moon was going to eat me," Dad said in all seriousness.

"Bwa-ha-ha!" I laughed. "No way! But that would never ever happen in a million years!"

"I know that *now*, but when I was young, I certainly didn't. Sometimes young people fear things simply because they don't understand them," he explained. "Once you experience more life situations, you'll be less afraid of... well, *everything*."

"I guess you're right," I said. "I just wish I could be a fearless superhero already. Life would be *so much* easier."

Dad got up and looked down the

hallway, making sure the coast was clear of eavesdroppers.

"Why don't you come along with Mom and me on patrol tonight?" Dad whispered.

"NO WAY!" Mom shouted from the hallway. She dropped what she was doing and came into my room. "I agree that Peter needs training and would benefit from watching us perform our duties, but tonight is just *not* the night," she said. "Bug Master is out there, and we need to be careful."

Normally I'd be champing at the bit to show the world my super skills—but not today. I wasn't about to risk getting attacked by a bunch of crazy insects. No way! So I just stayed quiet and let my parents talk it out.

"We've dealt with Bug Master before. He's a total nincompoop! We'll foil his evil plans and be back in time to watch a movie." Dad smirked.

BEEP BEEP BEEP!

Mom's trouble-alert device went crazy. "It looks like something buggy is happening at the library. We should head out," Mom said. She stared at me for a moment.

Here's where we part ways, I thought.

"All right, Peter, let's go," Mom commanded. "Stay on the sidelines and watch what we do. We have rules about this stuff, and you need to stick to them. This is serious business."

Yikes. That certainly didn't go the way I thought it would. Even though I was petrified, I had to be strong and confront my fears head-on. My parents would keep me safe. Still, I was both super horrified and pretty excited. My heart was pounding out of my chest!

My parents suited up while I put on my temporary costume. We took off like a bolt of lightning and soon arrived at the Boulder City Library, to find it covered in all kinds of fluttering insects—beetles, crickets, and flies, *oh my!*

"We're not here to harm these bugs," Dad

explained. "They're being mind-controlled and have no idea what they're doing. We need to keep them safe so we can study them later. Remember, Peter—there's no good reason for senseless violence. Always avoid a fight when you can."

"Got it!" I said.

Dad sprang into action, using his

flames to herd the
bugs away from
the library and
into the sky.

Once they got up high enough, Mom
sprayed them with a special mist so
they'd all fall asleep. Boulder City Pest
Control took it from there. They had
already set up special safety nets around
the library so that the sleeping bugs had
somewhere safe to fall.

Once the nets were
filled, they were taken
away. Now, *that* was
some teamwork! I was
so busy watching my

parents do their thing that I didn't notice a PRAYING MANTIS crawl onto the hedge next to me—until it chirped.

"Face your fear," I whispered to myself. But then the praying mantis took a step toward me with its weird green body.

My ice powers exploded out of me. Suddenly, I was surrounded by an ice igloo. I was totally safe from the bug.

When Mom and Dad were done cleaning things up, they came over to check on me. Dad used his flame powers to melt a window so they could see me.

"Hi," my muffled voice called out from inside the igloo. "I may have overreacted when I saw a bug."

"I'm impressed," Mom said. I couldn't see her face, but I think she was

smiling. "You protected yourself in a scary situation. Good job, Peter."

Dad was still thinking about work. "I don't get it. Bug Master didn't even show up! This was all a little too easy," he said.

"Think about it later, honey," Mom said. "Let's head home."

Home sounded good to me.

CHAPTER NINE
Dinner Interrupted

"Welcome to Pasta Palace," the waiter said. "Right this way. Your eating adventure awaits!"

The waiter brought us to our giant table. It was decked out with shiny silverware and everything. Since Mom and Dad had been so busy lately, they wanted to take the whole family out for a nice dinner.

"Right next to the window? Pretty fancy," Dad said, pulling out Mom's chair like a gentleman.

"What a great view of downtown," Mom said, strapping Ben into his booster seat.

"Who cares?" said Felicia, hopping onto her chair. She'd been sulking ever since we left the house.

"Yeah, my video games look better than this dumb old city," Gavin complained. Dad wouldn't let him bring his tablet, and he was annoyed.

"You know, some kids don't ever get to eat out in nice places like this," Grandpa said, wheeling up to the table. "They have to eat slop from a bucket! So be *thankful*."

We each grabbed a menu and began to search for yummy dinner options.

"Everything looks so good," Dad said, grinning from ear to ear. He loved having family dinners outside the house. Mostly because it meant he didn't have to cook.

The waiter came back with a special surprise. "To start you off, here's a bowl of our famous homemade spaghetti. Compliments of the chef!" he said, placing a big bowl of pasta on the table. Gavin was so excited, he stabbed his fork into the steaming spaghetti and gulped down a big bite. But then Felicia spotted something strange.

"Raisins aren't supposed to be in spaghetti," Felicia said. She poked at a little black ball peeking out from the noodles. It began to wiggle.

"That's not a raisin!" I screamed. Everyone in the restaurant turned and looked in our direction. Bugs began crawling out of the pasta and onto the table. My eyes got so big that I thought they might pop out. I was *petrified*.

Grandpa saw me and offered some words of wisdom. "Stay strong, Peter," he said. "Don't let your fears win! You can do this!" He swept the bugs away with his hand, and they fell to the floor, scattering in all directions. Then we heard a commotion coming from outside.

CRASH! BOOM! BLAST!

"What's going on out there?" Dad asked, peering out the window. "I don't see anything."

People in the restaurant started screaming when a giant spider woman ran by outside the window.

"Spidra!" Mom shouted.

"If *she's* here, that means Bug Master can't be far behind. He must have broken her out of jail," Dad said, taking a deep breath. "It's time to go to work."

Mom kissed my siblings and me on the forehead. "Dad, keep an eye on the kids," she said, handing Ben over. Grandpa gave a thumbs-up.

"Do NOT leave this restaurant," Dad said, looking right at Gavin and Felicia. They nodded in agreement. Dad put his hand on my shoulder. "Peter, keep an eye on your siblings, all right? And whatever happens, *stay inside*."

"Okay, Dad," I replied. My heart was racing again. I couldn't tell if it was because I was excited or scared, or maybe a little bit of both.

Mom and Dad ducked out to change into their superhero costumes. Soon they were out on the streets, ready for battle. Bug Master and Spidra were waiting for them.

"Back off!" Dad said, using his flames to keep the super-insect bad guys away from the restaurant. Gavin and Felicia were cheering for our parents—but I couldn't bear to watch. All I could think about were BUGS and how much they irked me. Some hero I turned out to be.

CHAPTER TEN
Bugs Get Bigger!

"DO SOMETHING, PETER!" Felicia said, grabbing at my shirt. "You want to be a hero so badly, shouldn't you be doing something?!"

"Peter, your powers are lame and you have no idea how to use them," Gavin chimed in. "But you *really* need to get out there and help our parents, dude!"

"Wait a minute!" I exclaimed. "Why don't *you* go out there and help? You've both got powers just like *I* do!"

Our parents were right outside the restaurant, facing off against Bug Master, Spidra, and their battle swarm of bugs. They had told us to stay put, and I was going to listen for once.

"Look!" Felicia shouted, pointing out the window. "The bugs are going away!"

She was right. The swarm of insects that covered the city was finally breaking apart and scattering in all directions. Our parents were winning! But *then* something even weirder happened: The bugs came back together to create one gigantic, super ugly BUG BEAST. It stomped over the buildings downtown.

There was no way around it—my

parents needed help now. It was time for Peter Powers to step up. But what could I possibly do? Especially when I was afraid of bugs?!

"Dagnabbit! I didn't want to have to

do this, but I guess it's up to ol' Dale to save the day once again," Grandpa said, tossing his napkin onto the table.

I guess it *wasn't* time for Peter Powers to step up to the plate. Grandpa had this one covered. I almost felt better.

"You kids watch over Ben, and I'll be back in a jiffy. Time to get my snack on!" Grandpa said, wheeling his chair outside. He slowly stood up as a pair of wings popped right out of his back. Grandpa flew high up into the air, getting dangerously close to the Bug Beast. He flipped his tongue out and snatched a mouthful of bugs right off that thing.

"Yummers!" Grandpa shouted. He

 couldn't get enough of those disgusting little insects. He kept gobbling them down like crazy.

Mom and Dad were battling Spidra nearby. Spidra blasted Mom with a burst of sticky webs. When Dad tried to help, she blasted him too. Spidra shot extra webbing on their hands so they couldn't move or use their powers. She even webbed their mouths shut.

Things weren't looking good. I was so afraid; I didn't know what to do. I felt like Peter *Powerless*.

CHAPTER ELEVEN
Spider Queen!

Spidra had trapped my parents in one of her webs while I just sat there like a lump. *If I was braver, I could save them*, I thought. How did I ever think I was good enough to be a superhero?

I had to do something, even if I got in trouble for it.

"We're leaving now," I told my siblings. "Gavin, grab Ben and be very careful with him. Felicia, grab my backpack and keep your mouth shut."

"Done," Felicia said. "But you don't have to be so rude about it."

I looked at the pile of bug-infested pasta on our table. *I'm glad I'm not paying for that*, I thought. But I reached into my pocket, pulled out a five-dollar bill, and placed it on the table as a tip. It was the last of my allowance money.

"Thanks for the service, sir!" I told the waiter.

"Uh, you're welcome?" the waiter replied. "Sorry about the, you know, bugs."

Gavin, Felicia, Ben, and I bolted from the restaurant and ducked into an alley nearby so we could watch Spidra in secret. We hid behind a dumpster and

listened
closely to
what she
was saying.

"Are you
comfortable?"
Spidra
asked Mom
and Dad.

"I always want to make sure that my
guests are taken care of properly." I hope
she wasn't expecting a real answer. Their
mouths were all webbed up, just like their
hands and feet.

"You two really cheesed me off, you know
that? You threw me in jail like some common

criminal. I'm SPIDRA, THE ARACHNID QUEEN! I belong on a beautiful throne of tarantulas, not in some dirty prison."

(If there's one thing I've learned in this line of work, it's that villains love to blather on and on about themselves. They'll reveal their entire plan if you let them!)

"The only reason I was at that elementary school was because they had the freshest flies in town. There's a tasty swarm of them right around the cafeteria dumpster. *That's* why I ripped everything apart. I had to find the very best ones. *Mmmmmm*," Spidra said, rubbing her belly. "Just thinking about it makes me hungry."

Mom tried to say something, but all

that came through the webbing was a mumble. Spidra ripped the webbing off her mouth so she could speak.

"WHAT?" Spidra shouted.

"You were destroying school property," Mom said, out of breath. "And when we tried to talk to you about it, *you* attacked us. *That's* why you were in jail."

"Oh," said Spidra, shrugging her shoulders. "My bad."

"We'll get you and your boyfriend—" Mom started. But Spidra slapped the webbing back into place.

"Enough talk. I don't need to listen to you," Spidra snapped. "I'm back and better than ever!"

"YAHOO!!!!" Grandpa's voice called out from the sky above. He chased the Bug Beast clear across town and back again, gulping down bugs and flying a mile a minute. I'd never seen Grandpa fly so fast. For an old-timer, he sure knew how to flap his wings.

"Time for the BUM RUSH!" Grandpa cried out, flying directly toward the Bug Beast.

"He's going to crash!" Felicia whispered worriedly.

"No, he's not. The creature isn't solid. It's made of thousands of bugs," I reassured her. "Now he's just having fun."

Grandpa flew straight through the

Bug Beast like a jet plane, breaking
it apart. Bugs flew in every direction,
with Grandpa chasing them off into the
distance.

"Go, Grandpa!" Gavin cheered.

"Keep your voice down, Gavin," I said.
"The last thing we need is for Spidra to
spot us."

With the Bug Beast destroyed, it was
time to reveal my master plan to rescue
Mom and Dad and save the city!

There was just one tiny little problem—
I didn't have a master plan yet.

CHAPTER TWELVE
A Villain Surprise!

"We have to do something…" I thought out loud. "But what can we do?"

"*We?* No way! I'm afraid of spiders," Felicia admitted. "Those long, hairy legs and big eyes. Just thinking about them makes me shiver. Are you happy now? The truth is out!"

"And I'm not going out there with all those scuzzy little bugs running around. They'll eat me! And I can't get eaten— I have a big game next week!" Gavin whined. "I'm scared of bugs too, okay?! Man, Peter, why did you make me admit that?"

"You're *both* afraid of bugs too?! Then why have you been giving me such a hard time?" I whispered angrily.

My siblings shrugged. They are the worst.

I was glad the truth was out, but they left me with one option: I was the only person left to save the day. Afraid or not, I had to help.

"I guess it's time for Peter Powers to take matters into his own hands," I said, standing proud before my siblings.

"It's so weird when you talk in the third person like that," Gavin said.

The mission was about saving my parents. This wasn't the time for fancy heroics. I was going to get in and get out without engaging Spidra in battle. She'd beat me in a second. I had to be sly.

I reached into my backpack and pulled out my temporary costume. It was an old hoodie that served as my superhero costume. Then I put on my eye mask.

"That hoodie is ugly," Felicia grumbled. "And it smells!"

I didn't care what it smelled like. I was a hero! I ran toward the battle.

"Peter!" Gavin called out. "Come back! You still need your mask."

"Oh yeah," I said, jogging back. Felicia handed me the mask, and I put it on.

But what could I do? Mom and Dad were still webbed up, but now Spidra was nowhere to be found. *Phew*, I thought.

"I really hope you know what you're doing," said Gavin.

"I'm going to sneak in, help our parents escape, then sneak out," I said, taking off toward Mom and Dad. I could feel my powers charging up. I was nervous but excited. Not only was I going to save my parents, I was also going to confront my fears head-on.

If even a single bug tried to get me, I'd blast it away with my ice-cube power.

I hate bugs so much, I thought, but I kept going. There was no turning back!

Just as I was about to reach my parents, something unexpected happened. The big swarm above began to come together again. It re-formed the giant Bug Beast! It was back and nastier than ever.

It stomped its big bug foot and blocked me from getting to Mom and Dad. The Bug Beast grabbed my hood and scooped me up into the air. I dangled there, unable to think of what to do. I was too scared.

"Well, well, well," Bug Master said. He appeared out of his swarm. "Who do we have here?"

CHAPTER THIRTEEN
Peter's Big Battle

I thought this was it. This was the end!

But then Bug Master squinted at me. "Wait a minute," he said to the Bug Beast, who was about to eat me. "He's just a little kid! Put him down!"

Once the Bug Beast dropped me on the ground, Bug Master said, "You shouldn't be out here. It's dangerous! What do you think you're doing, trying to take on super-villains? Wait! Don't answer. I don't care. I have my own problems to deal with."

"Why are you trying to destroy Boulder City?" I asked, using my forceful hero voice. I'd been working on it for a while.

"Ha! I don't want to destroy Boulder City. Are you crazy? It has the best parks in the entire country. And you know what parks have, right?" Bug Master asked.

"Trees?" I responded.

"Yes, and what else?" he asked again.

"Plants?" I offered.

"OKAY, SURE, AND WHAT ELSE?" Bug Master growled. He was getting angry now.

"Bugs," I guessed.

"BINGO!" Bug Master shouted, doing a little happy dance. "I really love insects. They're so cute and cuddly."

"No, they're not!" I said. "They're terrifying! Whenever someone tries to pick them up, they attack. They're scary, and I hate them!"

"Calm down, kid. You're trembling," Bug Master said. "Insects aren't as scary as you think. As a matter of fact, the only reason they *bug* you is because they're afraid. You're a big, dumb human being. If a tiny bug sees *you* coming for it, of course it's going to attack. It feels threatened. *You* are a *giant* to *it*."

As weird as it was to admit, Bug Master had a point. (Except the part about bugs being cute. I didn't understand *that* at all.)

"Now, go on. Get outta here. I've got

real problems!" Bug Master said, letting out a heavy sigh.

"Maybe I can help?" I asked. "I'm a superhero."

Bug Master sniffed at me. "Your costume really stinks," he said. "Oh, who cares! You wouldn't understand."

"Try me," I said.

"Well, my girlfriend, Spidra, and I are on the outs, and there's nothing to be done about it."

"So why did you break her out of jail?"

"I thought we had something special. I mean, I like bugs, and she *is* a bug. But I think she is using me—for my bugs.

She *eats* them. Did you know that?!
Spidra's not as nice a person as you
might think."

"I don't think she's a nice person *at
all*," I said. "Maybe you two should call it
quits? Sometimes things just don't work
out, you know?" I'd never been in a relationship, but I did see a lot of relationship
drama on Grandpa's TV shows.

"That's it! You're a genius!" Bug Master
paused. "But, uh...can you break up with
Spidra *for* me?"

"No way!" I said.

"Too late, she's here. Hi, sweetums!"
Bug Master said. Spidra was headed
in our direction. She must have been

shopping, because she had all kinds of bags with her. "She'll never wear any of that stuff," Bug Master whispered in my ear. "They don't make dresses that fit girls with two legs and six arms."

Spidra looked furious. "What's going on here?"

Bug Master pushed me forward and said, "This kid has something to tell you."

"Um, hello, Miss Spidra," I began, trembling with fear. "We haven't officially met, but you trapped my friends in some of your webs." I pointed to Mom and Dad. I was very careful not to reveal that they were actually my parents. It would have spoiled the whole secret-identity thing.

"Those are your friends, huh? They're annoying," Spidra said. "But what do *you* have to tell me?"

"Bug Master is breaking up with you!" I blurted out.

"ARGH! No one breaks up with me!" Spidra screamed. She shot web after web, cementing me and Bug Master in place. Neither of us could move.

Spidra crawled toward us and said, "Well, if I can't date you, then I guess I'll have to *eat* you, Bug Master. But I think I'll start with an appetizer...."

Spidra stalked toward me. I started screaming, "I don't want to be spider food! I don't want to be spider food!"

If I thought I was scared before, I was even more scared when she took off her mask. Spidra had the face of an actual spider!!!

"GAH!!!" I cried out in fear. Then I felt it happening. My ice power exploded!

It all happened so fast that—before I knew it—Spidra was totally frozen in a huge block of ice. *I did that*, I thought. It was awesome. I looked over at my parents, and they seemed relieved. Now we just had to get free.

CHAPTER FOURTEEN
Grounded Again

A few days ago, I never would have guessed that *I'd* be the one to take down Spidra and Bug Master. But today, I was able to tackle my fears—and it felt pretty great. (Even if my parents and I needed help from Gavin and Felicia to get us out of the webs.)

"Thanks, young mystery hero," Dad said, winking. We had to be very careful in front of the police once they arrived. No one knew that our entire family had powers. If anyone guessed our secret, we could all be in real trouble.

"You're very welcome!" I replied. "You two are the most amazing superheroes the world has ever seen. A child would be lucky to have such incredible people as parents."

"You're laying on the compliments a little thick," Mom whispered. "We can talk about all of this once we get home."

I really hoped they didn't ground me for disobeying their orders. "Got it!" I whispered back.

The ice covering Spidra was thawing, and she was shivering like crazy. "I hate this! Can someone get me a blanket, please?" she shouted at the cops.

"I'm not going to the same jail as *her*, am I?" Bug Master asked.

"If only you were that lucky!" Spidra sneered. "I can't bear to look at your face."

"Me?! *You're* the one who throws up acid on her food before she drinks it!"

Mom sighed. "Both of you, cut it out. We're taking you to separate prisons, and you'll never cross paths again."

As the cops loaded him into a prison truck, Bug Master said, "Thanks for breaking the news to Spidra, kid! And hey, I know you think bugs are scary, but don't let your fears guide you. Live and let live, I always say. We're all just creatures in the web of life!"

"Tell it to the judge," Dad said, closing the door on Bug Master.

As the cops took the villains away, Gavin, Felicia, and Ben waved at me from the alley. Grandpa Dale burped, his belly full of bugs. It was time to head home.

Once we returned to the house, things went right back to normal.

"I was definitely less scared than *you* were," Felicia said to Gavin.

"No way!" Gavin protested. "*You* were so scared, you probably peed your pants."

"I did NOT!" yelled Felicia.

"I said *probably*!" screamed Gavin.

I thought about butting in to remind them that it was me who charged into battle and saved everyone. But I didn't. Heroes don't need to rub their good deeds in people's faces—even if they're really super awesome good deeds that saved the whole city.

"Go get ready for bed, you two," Mom said. Gavin and Felicia did what they were told without complaining.

Grandpa was being quiet in the corner.

"Is everything okay, Grandpa?" I asked.

"Of course it is, Peter." He burped again. "I think I ate too many bugs. I need a nap." Grandpa wheeled off to his room for the night.

Mom and Dad sat me down on the couch.

"I'm grounded, aren't I?" I asked.

"Yes, you're grounded," Mom replied. "You disobeyed our instructions and involved yourself in a very dangerous situation." She paused for a second. "*But I'm very proud of you for trying to help. You stood up to your fears, looked them right in the face, and you didn't back down. That's what true heroes do.*"

She kissed me on the cheek and went to go check on Ben. Dad and I stayed up and talked for a bit. Actually, I did most of the talking, and he just listened.

"It was crazy, Dad. I thought I was going to fail because I was so afraid. But then all my nervousness went away, and my stomach unknotted itself. Do you think I'll ever be afraid of anything again?"

"Of course, Peter," said Dad. "There's always something out there to fear. What's important is that you face your fears. Don't let them win, no matter what you do. Fear can give us strength."

"I'll try my best," I said.

"You're doing great, son," Dad said, handing me a video game that he'd pulled out of his back pocket. "Don't tell your mom I let you have this." He patted me on the back and went to bed.

It can be hard sometimes when your parents are famous superheroes and your siblings are real pains in the rump. But tonight, I felt like the luckiest kid in the whole wide world.

CHAPTER FIFTEEN
High Dive, Take Two

"What's up, amigos?" I said, proudly strutting into the pool area wearing my borrowed pink-heart swim trunks. Last time I was afraid of what people thought, but this time I *knew* I looked like a million bucks.

"Peter, aren't you going to tell us about yesterday?" Chloe whispered. "We saw everything on the news."

I hadn't had a chance to tell Chloe and Sandro about my encounter with Bug

Master and Spidra just yet. They were really excited to hear about it.

"Yeah! When are you going to spill the beans? I want to know all about how you were able to fight off..." Sandro trailed off for a moment. "Well, you know, those little things that you hate talking about." He was afraid to say the word *bug*.

"Don't worry, Sandro. I conquered my fear of insects. I'm a new man! As a matter of fact, I think I'm feeling pretty fearless right now!"

"LINE UP, DUCKLINGS!" screamed Coach Winterbottom. I was so excited to get up on the diving board and show everyone how brave I was. There was no way I'd let fear get the best of me *this* time. Chloe, Sandro, and I were already standing at the front of the line, while Harry Hackney pushed his way to the front.

"I can't wait to show you how it's done, Powers," Hackney growled.

"Back of the line, Hackney," Coach Winterbottom growled. "No cutting in my class. First up is Peter Powers!"

I was on my way up the ladder and feeling pretty darn good. The higher I went, the more energized I became. Then I reached the middle of the ladder—and *it* happened. *I looked down.* Suddenly, I was frozen. I got that nervous feeling again. *I can do this*, I thought. *Be strong, Peter!*

"We don't have all day, Powers!" Hackney shouted.

"Put a cork in it! Watch and learn!" Sandro shouted back.

I looked over at Chloe. She mouthed

the words I needed to hear: *You've got this, Peter.*

I took a deep breath and continued up that ladder until I reached the very top. I stood there for a moment and looked around. A few days ago, I was so paralyzed by fear that I felt like I was going to lose my head. Now I felt stronger than ever.

So I walked to the end of the diving board and prepared to jump off. Suddenly, I tripped over my own two feet and fell forward. Instead of a perfect dive, I belly flopped in front of everyone. I splashed into the pool with a giant *SWACK!*

For the ten seconds I was underwater,
I couldn't help but laugh. Sure, I wish I
had gotten my high dive perfect, but that
wasn't the point. I DID IT! *That's* what
really mattered.

When I finally stuck my head above
water, I could hear my classmates laughing,
but I didn't care. They didn't know all the
crazy stuff I'd just been through. I rubbed

my eyes and looked over at Chloe and Sandro. I wasn't a famous superhero yet, but my best friends were each giving me a thumbs-up, and for now, that was all I needed.

Meet PETER POWERS!

A boy whose superpowers are a little different from the rest...

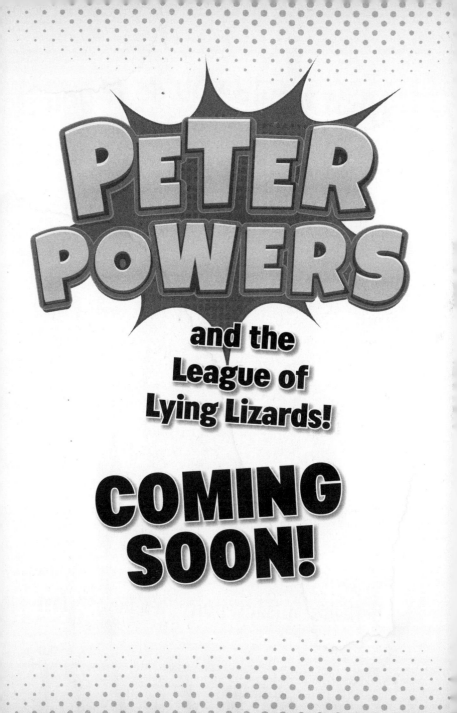

What would YOU do if you won the lottery?

Join the kids of Classroom 13 for their first misadventure in a new series!